This book is dedicated to Saoirse, Michael and Alfie –
the original Star Girl, Star Boy and Star Pet.
And also to:
Penelope for all she does
Marian for all she's done
And Sam for all he's doing! – J.J.M.

"Animals are such agreeable friends. They ask no
questions, they pass no criticisms." G. Eliot

"Grr...!" H. Hardpad

Text copyright © J. J. Murhall 1999
Illustrations copyright © Eleanor Taylor 1999

First published in Great Britain in 1999
by Macdonald Young Books
an imprint of Wayland Publishers Ltd
61 Western Road
Hove
East Sussex BN3 1JD

Find Macdonald Young Books on the internet at
http://www.myb.co.uk

The right of J. J. Murhall to be identified as the author
of this Work and the right of Eleanor Taylor to be
identified as the illustrator of the Work has been asserted
by them in accordance with the Copyright, Designs and
Patents Act 1988.

Designed and Typeset by McBride Design
Printed and bound by Guernsey Press

British Library Cataloguing in Publication Data Available

ISBN: 0 7500 2811 4

Star Pets on Stage

J. J. MURHALL
Illustrated by Eleanor Taylor

MACDONALD YOUNG BOOKS

STARRING:-
HILARY HARDPAD
RAYMOND HARDPAD
WOODRUFF BROWN

AND CO-STARRING:-
Brittany Burrows
Little Tone
Dallas Bigshot

AND FEATURING:-
Colin Curruthers
Quincy Truelove
Madame Swish
Miss Plummy

SPECIAL GUEST APPEARANCE:-
Ogden Bickerstaff as 'Henry the Fifth'.

Extras include: Gerbils, rabbits, hamsters, cats,
dogs, kittens and puppies. A pig and a parrot.

(No animal was harmed in the writing of this book –
not even Hilary Hardpad!)

Chapter One

Sweet Street was alive with the sound of animals. Barks, squeaks, squawks and snorts rose high above the buildings and weaved their way through the traffic jams of the city. A passing taxi driver pulled up and peered down the street.

5

"I see the animals are back in town," he remarked to his passenger. The man reading a newspaper on the back seat glanced up casually. The sight that met his eyes made him sit up in disbelief. Animals of every shape, size and colour were crammed into the narrow street. Some sat patiently on their suitcases whilst others said a tearful goodbye to their owners.

An enormous carthorse was having his nose blown on a handkerchief the size of a pillowcase. A lizard wearing mirrored sunglasses was practising a saxophone. Perched high up on a lamppost, squawking and flapping its wings, was a parrot singing opera.

The taxi driver glanced in his mirror at the amazed passenger.

"That's the YAPPS Academy," he stated proudly. "The Young Academy of Performing Pets. It's where pet owners send little Tiddles or Trixie if they think they've got what's known as 'Star Quality'. You must have seen the 'Peanut Butter Pup' on the telly."

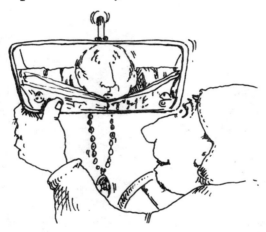

The man nodded. Everyone had seen *that* advert. It was the best one on TV.

"Well, he goes there," continued the driver. "And all of those animals waiting outside are the new pupils. That school's world famous, and every animal you see on TV, or in a film has usually passed through YAPPS."

9

He glanced down the street and frowned.

"Can't say that those two mangy-looking mutts lurking by the lamppost look like potential stars though," he added, pointing towards two skinny dogs who were watching the proceedings silently with dark, shifty eyes.

They were a breed known as a Tumbrel Terrier, extremely rare and certainly not very cute to look at. The larger one in particular had the face of a dog that should never be trusted. She was wearing a shiny plastic dog coat and a collar studded with small gold coins.

The smaller dog had the same coarse, wiry fur, but he had a kinder face that glanced nervously up at the dog beside him. They were sister and brother and their names were Hilary and Raymond Hardpad. Raymond, the younger one, wanted to be a magician, and was quite skilled at it. But, the only talent Hilary possessed was to be the most horrible hound in the world, especially to Raymond. She'd even snapped his wand in two and eaten it once. But that was typical of Hilary. She was jealous, spiteful, and very, very, big-headed.

At exactly nine o'clock, the kennel-shaped clock perched high on top of the roof began to chime. The massive doors opened and Madame Swish, the principal of the school, stepped outside.

"Welcome to YAPPS," she announced, smiling broadly.

"First you will be allocated your rooms. The largest animals will take the first floor where the bedrooms are the biggest, medium-sized pupils are on the floor above and the tiniest animals will have the cosy attic rooms at the very top of the building. After you've settled in, there will be a tour of the school. So please form an orderly line and follow me inside."

As she walked back inside, the eager new
pupils, in a flurry of fur and feathers, clambered
up the steep steps and tumbled in after her.
Hilary Hardpad followed slowly behind, wrinkling
up her nose in disgust as an excitable puppy left
a tell-tale puddle on the top step.

14

"Savages. I'm surrounded by savages," she
declared, staring disdainfully down at her brother
as he struggled valiantly with their entire luggage.
"Hurry up, Raymond. I want to make sure that
I get the best bedroom in the school. Our owner
doesn't give heaps of money to this dump for
nothing. I'm not sharing with anyone... Especially
not a rabbit or a guinea-pig. They always smell
of hay."

Her expression hardened as a pretty grey rabbit with short delicate ears hopped towards her. She was pulling a suitcase on wheels and carried a straw handbag with a carrot embroidered on the front. Raymond noticed that she was wearing a pair of tiny white high-heeled shoes on her back feet. The rabbit smiled up at Hilary with wide green eyes and put out a front paw.

"Hello," she said, "My name's Brittany, and I'm your new room-mate. Ooo! Isn't it simply exciting," she giggled. "I simply can't believe I'm here. I simply didn't have a clue what to pack. I've had to leave most of my shoes at home and could only bring my favourite eighty-four pairs. I simply *love* shoes".

Suddenly, a mobile phone rang from the depths of her enormous handbag and Brittany pulled it out.

"Excuse me. But I simply must answer this," she smiled.

"Hello. Oh it's *you*, honeybun," she squealed. She put a paw over the mouthpiece and whispered, "It's one of my sisters." Hilary rolled her eyes and growled under her breath as Brittany chatted away, using the word 'simply' about a hundred times. When she'd finished, Brittany put her mobile back and picked up her luggage.

"Sorry about that. It was Tallulah, calling from the aromatherapist. We like to keep in touch. I've got seven sisters: April, Lark, Felicity, Tallulah, Babs, Melody and Candice. I'm the baby of the family. They've all been to YAPPS and Lark stars on TV in the vet series *Pets in Peril*. She's simply amazing in it. Anyway, Madame Swish says we're to meet in the lobby in half an hour, so I simply must go and unpack. See you upstairs, Hilary."

And she hopped off, smiling at everyone as she bounced up the sweeping staircase.

"She seems very nice," said Raymond,
watching as Brittany answered her mobile again,
this time to Candice calling from the health club.

"Nice?" snapped Hilary throwing her brother
an angry look. "NICE! She's a half-wit and a
bubble-brain, *and* she smells of hay. I don't
know how I'm going to put up with her and that
blasted mobile ringing night and day." And with
that, she stormed off after Brittany who was now
talking to Melody, calling from the cruise ship
where she worked as a cabaret singer.

Raymond sat down on Hilary's vanity case and sighed. His sister could be such a pain. But Raymond's face brightened as a friendly-faced monkey swung across the chandeliers towards him, jumped down and handed him his room key. "Hiya. The name's Tony, but everyone calls me Little Tone," declared the monkey bouncing excitedly up and down on his heels.

"We're sharing a room together. Let me give you a hand." Raymond watched in amazement as Little Tone proceeded to pile case after case on top of his head. Balancing them with difficulty, Little Tone waddled off with Raymond in hot pursuit. Things were looking up. He'd found a friend and best of all he didn't have to room with Hilary. She'd have stopped him doing his magic tricks and she snored like a family of warthogs with a heavy cold.

Chapter Two

"And here we have the modern dance class," announced Madame Swish throwing open the door into yet another enormous, airy room.

The new pupils shuffled inside, watching in amazement as various animals dressed in leotards, leg warmers and headbands leapt across the floor to some very weird-sounding music.

The tour of the school that morning had been hectic. It had already taken in a ballet class, a horse tap-dancing class and a singing lesson. They'd also visited the wardrobe department and watched a parrot being coached in Spanish by the voice teacher, Miss Plummy.

Brittany nudged Hilary as the pupils bent and stretched into peculiar positions on the dance floor. "Look at him over there. Isn't he *simply* the cutest thing," she whispered pointing to a ginger guinea-pig doing the splits. His headband had fallen over his eyes, but Hilary recognized him straight away.

"Well, well, well. If it isn't Woodruff Brown," she sneered.

24

"We used to be in the same pet shop ages ago. I wondered what had happened to him. Woodruff wants to be a stand-up comedian, but that snivelling little ginger whinger is far too wet to make it to the big time." She pointed to a battered leather bag and a worn blanket lying in the far corner.

"That bag contains all his vitamin pills and the blanket is his pride and joy. He worries about two things: his health and losing that moth-eaten cover."

Brittany smiled as Woodruff took off his big black square-framed glasses and wiped his face lovingly on his blanket. "Well, I think he's simply divine," she declared. Hilary stared at Brittany distastefully as Madame Swish hustled everyone out and on to the next class.

"He's the wettest guinea-pig that ever lived," she snapped, following the others down a long corridor. Madame Swish put a finger to her lips as they passed the music room, where a violin exam was taking place.

Quincy Truelove, a lime-green lizard, took off his sunglasses and peeped through the window. Music was his passion and he couldn't wait to join the school orchestra. Next, Madame Swish led them into a dark studio where some third-year students were rehearsing a play. It involved a lot of animals dressed in sheets speaking in a very strange language. A gerbil called Ogden pushed past Hilary to get to the front. He watched wide-eyed and totally spellbound.

"They're reading Shakespeare – England's finest playwright," declared Madame Swish, smiling down at Ogden.

"It's ace," replied the gerbil excitedly. "When can I have a go?"

"It sounds like a load of rubbish to me. I can't understand a word that they're saying," declared Hilary sneering, as one of the actors made a speech about a kingdom and a horse.

Glaring at Hilary, Madame Swish led everyone out, down a long winding staircase, and into the basement workshops. A group of animals were painting scenery in one room and, in the other, stage make-up lessons were taking place.

Little Tone waited for Raymond as he held back. "Are you OK, mate?" he asked, looking concerned.

"I was just remembering when I used to live with my owner, Mrs Bargestorm," replied Raymond sadly. "I had my own dog basket and loads of squeaky toys to play with. And then my sister Hilary went and spoilt it all – again. The reason we're here is not because we're potential Star Pets; it's because Mrs Bargestorm gives vast donations to the school fund and couldn't take care of us any more."

"Why not?" asked Little Tone.

"Mrs Bargestorm is ancient. She's as deaf as a post and has a walking stick," Raymond sighed. "One day she bent over to pick it up and Hilary bit her on the backside. My sister loves two things: one is wood and the other's a nice chunky bottom."

Little Tone nodded sympathetically. He'd heard rumours about Hilary and her wayward teeth.

Set and costumes

The tour took longer than expected because Ogden got lost backstage. When he'd been found (he was trying on some costumes), the principal announced that after lunch there would be an informal acting class.

"We have a very important person arriving this afternoon," declared Madame Swish.

"Dallas Bigshot is flying over from Hollywood to audition a second-year student for a part in his next film." Some of the animals gasped, recognizing the name of America's greatest film director.

Ogden put up his paw. "Who's he going to audition, Miss?" he asked eagerly.

"He's extremely talented, and some of you may have spotted him in the modern dance class earlier," replied Madame Swish. "He was wearing glasses, has red hair, and his name is Woodruff Brown." And she headed off towards the staff room. The animals chattered excitedly amongst themselves as they made their way to the canteen. The first day at YAPPS was turning out to be even more thrilling than they had ever dreamed of.

Dallas Bigshot was coming to town. He could turn you into a Star Pet overnight!

"Are you coming to lunch Hilary?" asked Raymond, when everyone had gone.

Hilary didn't reply. She was too busy chewing on a chair leg. Raymond looked anxiously around as Hilary prised her teeth away from the leg, spat a shower of splinters all over the floor and glared at her brother.

"How dare she praise that gormless goggle-eyed guinea-pig!" Hilary seethed. "There's no way that Woodruff Brown is going to become famous before I do."

Raymond nervously nibbled his nails. His sister had that mad gleam in her eye that she used to have in the pet shop. 'Bonkers' Hardpad, she'd been known as back then. Hilary's teeth began to grind and her top lip started to curl.

"Woodruff Brown can't even take a shower without that manky mat of his," she growled softly. "Once I get my paws on it, he'll be history and then *I'll* become the greatest Star Pet that this crummy school has ever seen. The biggest in the world. Bigger than that labrador pup on *Beaches, Barbies and Babes*. Follow me Raymond. We've no time to lose!"

"But where are we going, Hilary? I haven't had my lunch yet," replied Raymond hurrying after her. Hilary ignored him as she trotted across the foyer towards the costume department, her toenails clipping noisily on the shiny marble floor.

This was a sound that the other animals at YAPPS would soon begin to dread. For Hilary Hardpad never, ever, clipped her toenails.

"All the better to scratch you with," she'd threaten. "And to tear your favourite toy to bits as well," she'd add nastily.

Chapter Three

Woodruff Brown paced the room nervously.
He had a bottle of smelling salts in his pocket
and in his paw was his well-nibbled joke book.
Only Woodruff didn't feel like laughing. He felt
more like hiding under his precious blanket. His
audition was in half an hour and he was feeling
very, very tense.

As he turned the page, there was a sharp tap at the door that made him jump. A shrill voice called out, "Open up. Laundry please." Woodruff put his book down on the bed beside his blanket and opened the door. Standing before him were two scrawny dogs wearing the most peculiar clothes. The larger one wore a horrible frilly dress and a massive blonde wig that wobbled every time she spoke. The smaller dog was dressed from head to paw in old-fashioned golfing gear. He wore baggy trousers, a diamond-patterned sweater and an enormous cap that looked like a pancake. He sidled into the room pulling a trolley with a bin liner attached to it. Woodruff frowned. Their faces looked familiar, but in the ridiculous costumes he couldn't place them.

40

"We've come for your dirty duvets," declared the bigger dog. Marching over to Woodruff's bed, she hastily gathered up his covers and bundled them into the sack. Then, without a word, she turned around and marched back out with the smaller dog puffing and panting behind her.

"But what about my room-mate's sheets?" asked Woodruff, politely helping him. "And how come you're dressed like that? Cleaners normally wear overalls, don't they?"

"They're in the wash," replied the dog in a dress, breaking into a trot along the corridor. "We'll be back for the rest later. I'm off for a tea break now." And she disappeared around the corner so fast her wig flew off. Woodruff shrugged, closed the door behind him and stared across at his bare bed.

Then he frowned down at the floor as he realized something was wrong.

His eyes began to widen in disbelief. The two most important things in his life, his joke book and the security blanket that he'd had since the day that he was born, had disappeared. He opened the door quickly and peered down the long corridor. It was empty... except for the wig lying sprawled on the carpet.

Woodruff closed the door in a panic and reached for his bag. Pulling out a selection of vitamins he munched on them anxiously.

What was he to do? Without his blanket he was nothing. Just another stand-up comedian on the road to nowhere. He slumped down on the floor, dejected. His audition was in fifteen minutes – he might as well give up now. Then suddenly, from beneath the door came a rustling sound as a piece of paper was shoved under it.

Woodruff picked it up and read:

Woodruff pushed his glasses up his nose and studied the list of jokes. They went from bad to worse to downright terrible and back again. If he told these jokes he wouldn't stand a chance, but Woodruff knew he had no choice.

A few minutes later, thinking only of his cherished blanket, Woodruff hurried towards the main hall where the auditions were taking place. Ignoring the calls of "Good Luck, Woody," Woodruff entered through the side door that led to the stage and climbed up on to it. With his knees knocking, he turned to face Dallas Bigshot and his assistants. Spotlights beamed down on him. Woodruff began to sweat.

"OK, Woodruff. Do your stuff," a voice called out.

Woodruff glanced in the wings. To his astonishment, he saw Hilary Hardpad peeping around the curtain. She was wearing her distinctive dog coat again and his blanket was clamped firmly between her teeth. Woodruff knew she could tear it to shreds and swallow it in an instant. The guinea-pig gulped. It was now or never. He cleared his throat and began.

"I say, I say, I say. What do you call a girl standing between two goal posts? – ANNETTE!"

49

Silence. Woodruff coughed nervously.

"What lies at the bottom of the sea and shivers? – A NERVOUS WRECK!"

From the back of the hall you could hear a pin drop. Not a sound, not a murmur, not even a teeny-weeny snigger. Woodruff continued with his terrible jokes, wishing that the floor would swallow him up. When he'd finished, he waited anxiously. Finally, Dallas Bigshot stood up.

Woodruff's lip began to quiver and he wrung his paws together, waiting to be told off. But instead Mr Bigshot started to smile and then he began to clap.

"Well kid, in all my days as the world's greatest director, I have NEVER EVER heard such terrible jokes." Woodruff's shoulders slumped and he turned to walk away, utterly humiliated.

"STOP!" cried Mr Bigshot chomping on his cigar. "It was BRILLIANT! Comic genius, in fact. How did you manage to tell those jokes without bursting into tears? Over the years I've auditioned animals and humans who can tell hilarious jokes. But Woodruff, baby, I've heard them all before. You're different. The best guinea-pig comedian I've ever seen. I'm casting a big part in my new film for a character who tells really bad jokes. You're perfect! Whadda you say, my little furry friend? You wanna go to Hollywood?"

Woodruff was aghast. But before he could reply, Hilary tossed the blanket to one side and charged on to the stage. Her face was like thunder.

"Are you mad?" she glared at the director. "Woodruff can't possibly be a movie star. He's far too short and weedy. You need someone like me, Mr Bigshot. A classic beauty." And she bared her teeth and fluttered her eyelashes, which only made her look worse. Dallas Bigshot shook his head in disbelief.

"You're joking! You look like an extra from a horror film!" he laughed, bending over to pick up his briefcase. Hilary's eyes narrowed. She'd seen this view somewhere before. Licking her lips she remembered tasty old Mrs Bargestorm. In an instant Hilary leapt off the stage, lunged towards him and pounced, sinking her teeth into his ample bottom. Mr Bigshot shot up in the air like a firework as Hilary raced off with half his underpants between her teeth.

"How dare you bite the butt of the world's most famous film director!" he roared, holding on to what was left of his trousers. "Your career's over! You'll never work again! I'll have you expelled! I'll have you sent to Battersea Dogs' Home!" And he shook his fist as Hilary, the coins on her collar tinkling furiously, disappeared through the exit doors.

Meanwhile, Woodruff hurried over to his discarded blanket, picked it up and held it to his chest like a long lost friend.

"I'm sorry about Hilary's behaviour. She's always been a handful," he said, watching as Mr Bigshot's assistants fussed over him. "Can I still come to Hollywood?"

"You bet my bitten backside you can," replied the director firmly.

Woodruff held his blanket up. "Could I bring this though? I'm much funnier with it."

Dallas Bigshot let out an almighty roar. He felt better already. "What a joker!" He grinned at his assistants. "What a STAR PET!"

Chapter Four

Next morning all the new pupils gathered in the main hall for assembly.

Madame Swish and the other tutors stood up on the stage surveying the sea of faces.

"I'm pleased to announce that Woodruff Brown has gone to Hollywood," announced the principal proudly.

Brittany smiled at Hilary, who sank lower down in her seat. She wanted to keep out of Madame Swish's way for a while. She'd been punished enough already. Having to pack Woodruff Brown's suitcases before he'd caught his plane had been bad enough. (He'd been so shaky he hadn't even been able to fold his swimming trunks properly, the wimp!) But then, because he'd bitten his nails so badly, she'd had to give him a manicure as well!

This was not the way to treat a potential Star Pet and she'd waved good riddance to the gawky guinea-pig. At least the principal had managed to calm Mr Bigshot down though. Hilary had shuddered at the thought of having to sew up his underpants. They were so gigantic it would have taken her at least a week! However, the terrible terrier had gone on report for costume stealing, bottom biting and joke tampering.

"Isn't that simply a dream come true?" whispered Brittany as her mobile went off. It was Babs calling from the hairdressers. The principal was extremely annoyed and sent Brittany to wait outside.

"*If* I may continue," said Madame Swish sternly. "For most of you, it will be a long hard climb to the top. Some will make it. Others will simply go back to their owners."

The animals stared eagerly up at her, each with their own dreams of stardom. Raymond thought of becoming a magician with an assistant called Margery. Ogden thought of the RSC – the Rodent Shakespeare Company. Everyone longed to be famous, from the smallest hamster to the biggest carthorse. By paw or claw or hoof, no one, not even Hilary Hardpad, was going to stop them. Being an animal was OK and being a pet was even better, but to become a STAR PET, well, *that* was something *really* special.

So, the next time you're walking your dog, or feeding your cat, or cleaning out the hamster's cage at school, take a closer look at them.

Do you think they've got what it takes to become a STAR PET?

Because I bet *they* do!

Look out for more Star Pet adventures:

Star Pets on Screen

It's panic stations at YAPPS (the Young Academy of Performing Pets) when Brittany, the air-headed bunny, gets the chance to appear in a TV soap commercial. Brittany thinks that she will become a soap star, but she hasn't bargained for slippery Hilary Hardpad, a massive shoe sale and two all-action stunt cats...

Star Pets Make it Big

It's Top of the Pets time at YAPPS when the animals form a band. With a lizard on saxophone, a terrier on drums and a gerbil dancing on the keyboards, they look set for stardom. But is fame and fortune all it's cracked up to be? And who is the mysterious groupie?

Star Pets in the Spotlight

The end-of-term show is the chance for the pupils at YAPPS to shine. With tap-dancing horses and a rabbit dressed as a pig, the stage is set for a great show. But with meddling Hilary Hardpad in charge of sound effects, things are sure to go with a bang!

For more information about Star Pets, write to:
The Sales Department, Macdonald Young Books
61 Western Road, Hove, East Sussex
BN3 1JD